0/23

written by
Erica Simone Turnipseed

illustrated by
Kara Bodegón-Hikino

BIGGER THAN ME

atheneum
A CAITLYN DLOUHY BOOK
Atheneum Books for Young Readers • New York London Toronto Sydney New Delhi

ATHENEUM BOOKS FOR YOUNG READERS
An imprint of Simon & Schuster Children's Publishing Division
1230 Avenue of the Americas, New York, New York 10020
Text © 2023 by Erica Simone Turnipseed
Illustration © 2023 by Ma. Carmen Amparo Bodegón
Book design by Lauren Rille © 2023 by Simon & Schuster, Inc.
ATHENEUM BOOKS FOR YOUNG READERS is a registered trademark of Simon & Schuster, Inc.
Atheneum logo is a trademark of Simon & Schuster, Inc.
For information about special discounts for bulk purchases, please contact Simon & Schuster Special Sales at
1-866-506-1949 or business@simonandschuster.com.
The Simon & Schuster Speakers Bureau can bring authors to your live event.
For more information or to book an event, contact the Simon & Schuster Speakers Bureau
at 1-866-248-3049 or visit our website at www.simonspeakers.com.
The text for this book was set in Catalina Clemente.
The illustrations for this book were rendered digitally with custom brushes.
Manufactured in China
0523 SCP
First Edition
10 9 8 7 6 5 4 3 2 1
CIP data for this book is available from the Library of Congress.
ISBN 9781665900324
ISBN 9781665900331 (ebook)

For Lena, Kellis,
and all the children whose hearts and hands
hold words that reach up to the sky
—E. S. T.

To my nieces, Isla and Luna,
and the kids I grew up with
—K. B.

Words rush in.

Big words.
Shadows that Luna can see
but not catch.

climate

immigration

Quaranti

Big words with big meanings
boom through the house
and clang in Luna's ears.
Words like "pandemic" and "homelessness."
"Inequality" and "immigration."

injustice

homel

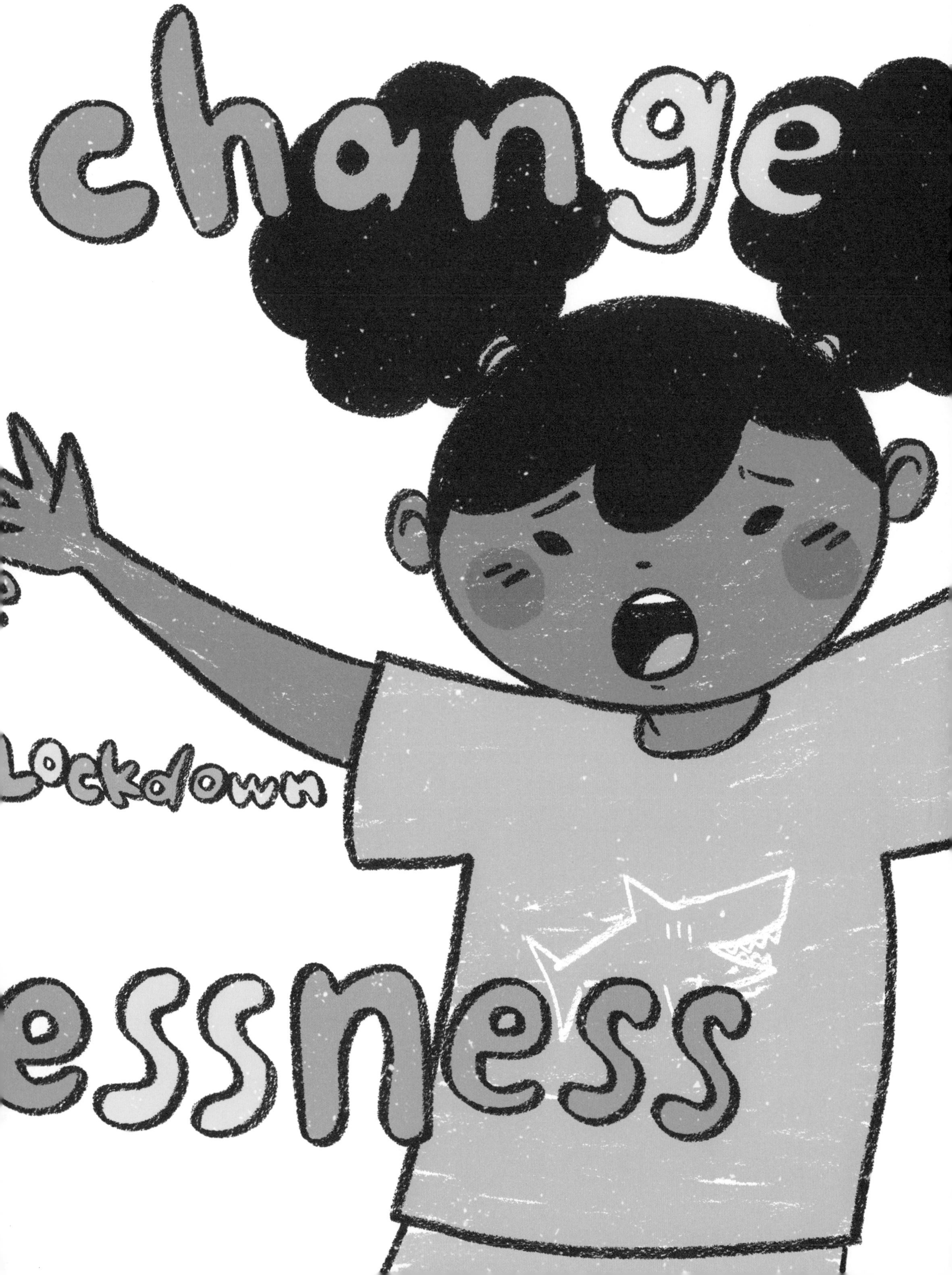
change
Lockdown
essness

Zion counts the syllables over and over again,
the words a wad of gum too big to chew.
Luna and Zion wonder if these words
are big enough to swallow them up.

Luna mouths one silently as she
assembles wooden letter blocks into a wobbly stack
high above her head.
Zion cranes his neck all the way up
but can't see the top.

Luna measures her word towers with hands held wide,
but she stumbles.
Zion tries to catch the falling blocks,
but he fumbles.
And all the big words land in a jumbled heap.

These words are so big, and they are so small.
They feel as small as the teardrops on their faces.
Luna and Zion stare at the tumble of blocks,
letters that are no longer words,
their meanings scattered in
a pile of frustration at their feet.

Zion taps his toe and recalls how his first big puzzle seemed like a hundred pieces of nonsense until Luna helped him figure it out.

Luna chomps her bubble gum and remembers the plastic jar Zion gave her to store all her chewed wads.

Zion and Luna rescue an abandoned shopping cart
and begin to collect this and that,
every discarded thing that needs a new job.
They've got big plans in mind.

But their hands are smaller than their plans,
and their dreams are bigger than their bodies.
They can't reach everything they see
or carry everything they find.

Zion sees Gadget Guy,
who makes the best gadgets in the neighborhood.

Luna waves over Pascale and Pricilla,
the tallest kids she knows.

Just then Hannah and Ha-yoon scooter past
before turning around and scootering back.

Daquan and Daisy look out their kitchen window and hop out to help.

Then come Mark, Shimon and Larry, Taiwo and Kehinde.

They maneuver milk crates,
repurpose used paint cans,
and salvage old shoe heels that have no shoe at all.

Now the cart brims to overflowing,
full of odds and ends, bits and pieces.

Others join the brigade—
a makeshift kids' parade!

Vijay, Wilder, Sara, and Cinque,
Ahanu and Bolade,
Madelyn and Catherine,
Nina, Juanita, and Alfred,
Samar and Dante.

Together
they paste, tack, and tape.
They loop rubber bands and tie jump ropes,
so many hands busy.

Big words sprout up from the street,
powerful words magnified by the sun.
Friends hopscotch to the beat of each syllable.

Elders spell words with their Scrabble tiles.
They construct word skyscrapers that touch the clouds.

Words so big,
bigger than Luna,
bigger than Zion,
but not too big to grasp.

Big, but not too big.

Because everyone is carrying them
in their hearts,
and in their hands.

Luna chants them,
and her voice echoes like a chorus.

Zion blows oodles of bubbles
that drift up, up, up
and form a crown
atop the big words.

The kids honor heroes
who fill the world with words like
"integrity," "human rights," and "conscience."
They make their words a cheer:
"Empathy and action!"

They honor the brave humanitarians who fill the world with words like "generosity" and "perseverance"!

They join their voices and trumpet,
"Joy and laughter!"
These are big words we *all* need,

kindness

big words that lift our gazes
and puff out our chests.
Words that float high over our heads.
"Freedom and hope!"

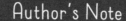

Author's Note

The seed of this story took root in the wake of several historic events: the coronavirus pandemic, the country's racial reckoning, and the passing of civil rights champion and "conscience of Congress" Rep. John Lewis. Even as my husband and I reeled from the gravity of current events, we saw that our children also were struggling to make sense of so many big words and issues. *Bigger Than Me* is my gift to all the children and families doing the same thing.

Who's in the mural?

The mural on pages 34-35 depicts six individuals whose big words and actions have made our world kinder and more just. From left to right, they are:

Representative John Lewis (1940-2020), who was a congressman in the U.S. House of Representatives, a human rights activist, and a leader of the civil rights movement

Malala Yousafzai (1997-), who is an activist from Pakistan focused on girls' and women's educational access

Maria A. Ressa (1963-), who is a Filipino and American investigative journalist and defender of freedom of expression and integrity in politics

Rigoberta Menchú (1959-), who is an Indigenous Guatemalan rights activist, author, and spokesperson for Indigenous people worldwide

Dr. Wangari Maathai (1940-2011), who was a Kenyan political activist and pioneer in linking environmental conservation to human rights

Fred Rogers (1928-2003), who was a Presbyterian minister and American television host and producer of the groundbreaking children's program *Mister Rogers' Neighborhood*